Bumble  Bear

ROLL OUT THE BARREL

WRITTEN BY JAMES HOFFMAN   ILLUSTRATED BY JOHN SANDFORD

Dedicated to one of my cubs,
Jonathan Scott Peter.
J.D.H.

For Andrew Smith,
a large chip off the crusty old block.
J.S.

Bumble Bear loved honey. So did his cubs, Wear and Tear. Lately, howev[er]
the honey jars in the Bear family's cottage were all empty. Bumble Bear v[as]
always fishing for new ways to get honey, but his plans always got away.

One day, Wear and Tear were talking about their father's love of honey. Of course, Wear and Tear liked honey too, but they also liked lots of other things cooked by their mother, Gwendolyn Bear. She made delicious raspberry pie and fish cakes and wonderful hickory-nut muffins and gooseberry jam. The Bears' cupboard wasn't bare!

But Bumble Bear thought *only* about honey. "Honey, honey, honey," said Wear. "That's all he *ever* thinks about!" "And everything he does to get honey goes wrong," said Tear. "Dressing like a bee—building a new hive. If he wants honey so badly, why doesn't he just *ask* for it?"

Then Wear and Tear looked at each other and giggled. They had their *own* idea about how to get honey! This time, *they* would be the ones to decide what to do next!

Wear and Tear asked Gwendolyn Bear for an empty honey jar. Then they washed their hands and faces and put on their best clothes. Tear tied his own tie, and Wear borrowed a little of her mother's honeysuckle perfume.

When they stepped outside, it was a beautiful day. The meadow was filled with flowers opening to the sun. Wear and Tear could hear the bees buzzing around their hive down in the meadow. Holding their empty jar, off to the hive they went.

When they arrived, Wear tapped lightly and politely on the hive. "Mr. and Mrs. Bee," she said, "Could we trouble you for a little honey?" "Please," added Tear with his nicest smile.

A low hum arose from the hive, growing louder and louder until the buzz filled the cubs' ears. The bees were telling Wear and Tear to help themselves. Tear reached carefully into the hive and took a piece of honeycomb. Wear said, "Thank you very much!"

That night at dinner, there was honey on the table for the first time in weeks. "Where on earth did this come from?" asked Gwendolyn Bear, so Wear and Tear told their story. Bumble Bear listened with his mouth open in surprise. When the cubs were through talking, Bumble Bear said, "You simply *asked* for it?" He thought for a moment and then said cunningly, "So will I!"

The next morning, Bumble Bear grabbed an empty honey jar from the cottage kitchen and headed for the door. "Wait a minute!" he thought, a smile spreading on his face. "Why not something a little bigger? A can? A bucket? A washtub?" Bumble Bear pictured each one. None of them was *quite* big enough. "Why not a barrel?" he thought.

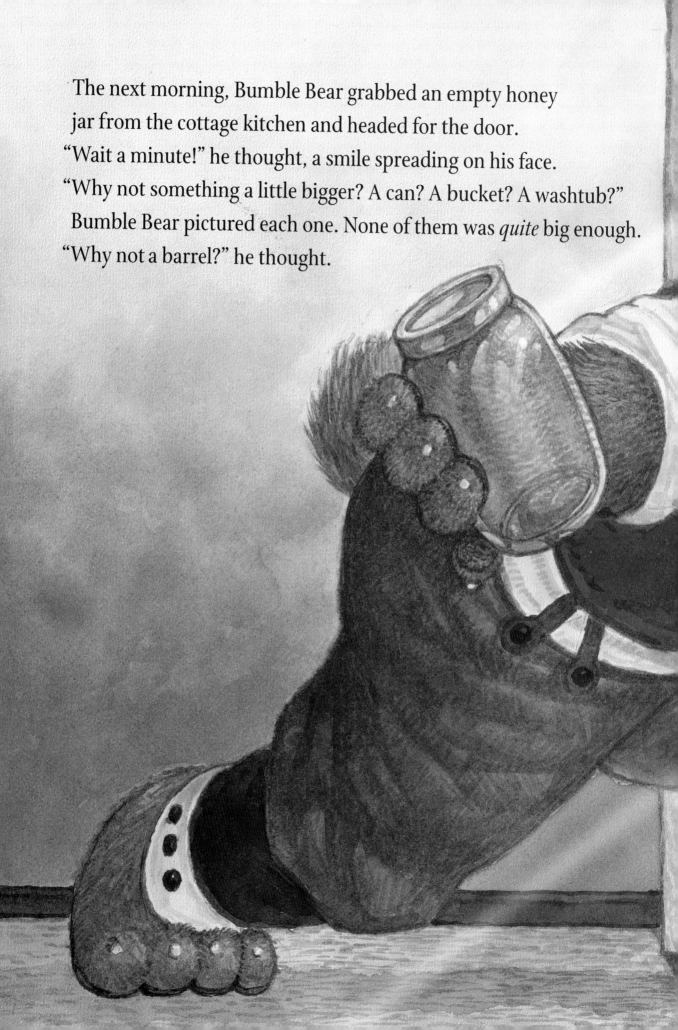

There was a barrel by the downspout of Honey Hill Cottage.
Bumble Bear laid it on its side and started to roll it across the meadow.
As he rolled, he created a song of his own making: "A barrel of honey,
buzz-buzz-buzz-buzz! A barrel of honey, please-please-please-please!"
Then he sang, "*Roll out the barrel! We'll have a honey of a time!*"

Bumble Bear knocked on the hive when he arrived. But he didn't tap politely — he pounded! When there was no answer, he pounded again, but even harder this time. "This is so simple!" he thought. As he stood waiting outside the hive, he began to sing, *"Roll out the barrel! I want some honey, a ton!"* Suddenly, the bees began humming along, but the tune didn't sound as sweet. *"Roll out the barrel! We'll have that bear on the run!"*

And just as suddenly, Bumble Bear was surrounded by angry bees who wanted to teach him some manners. They buzzed. They swarmed. They stung! Bumble Bear jumped. He jumped right into the barrel, shedding his clothing that was full of bees.

Bumble Bear had bumbled again. He rolled all the way home
and then climbed out of the barrel still in his underwear.
"Another honey of a plan has crumbled!" he grumbled.
"Roll out the barrel *indeed!*"

That same night, though, Bumble Bear was back in his den, studying and thinking, looking at the signs about bees and hives and honey on his wall. He thought, "Sooner or later, I'll think of a plan to get honey that I *won't* fumble!"

Wear and Tear walked giggling into the den. They told Bumble Bear how they'd visited the hive to pick up his clothing and sang "Honeybumble Rose" to calm the honeybees. The bees had shared some honeycomb with them for each stanza.

That would make Bumble Bear feel better at breakfast!